WHO?

THE BEGINNING

M AJAY DEEPU

Contents

Preface

I am the youngest writer of suspense and horror stories in my school. I like to spend my time with writing some different stories. I was born in 18th June 2006 in Visakhapatnam, Andhra Pradesh. I got my inspiration from the gratest author William Shakespeare and Ruskin Bond. My friends, teachers,parents encouraged me to write these type of stories.

Shakespeare

Ruskin Bond

CHARACTER

Rakesh : A young ,great detective

Angelina : Bank manager in HSBC and lover of Rakesh

John Carter : Old fiend of Rakesh and who has grudge on Rakesh

Mrs.Deepthi : Class teacher of Rakesh when he was studying in his school

Mrs.Marry : School pricinpal when Rakesh was studying

Jake : Friend of Rakesh and a scientist

CHARACTER INTRODUCTION

Rakesh : A young ,great detective

Angelina : Bank manager in HSBC and lover of Rakesh

John Carter : Old fiend of Rakesh and who has grudge on Rakesh

Mrs.Deepthi : Class teacher of Rakesh when he was studying in his school

Mrs.Marry : School pricinpal when Rakesh was studying

Jake : Friend of Rakesh and a scientist

CHAPTER ONE

THE BEGINNING!

It was around 10:30 in the night. It was so dark and rakesh was was returning to his home from his office. Dogs were barking in a distance. Street lights are swaying due to cool breezes. He reached home, he laid his bag on a cushion and removed his tie and he hooked his hat to the hangar and went to fresh up. After freshing up sat on his bed and opened his laptop and when he opens whatsapp he saw that Angelina had sent some pics...

Angelina : pics[selfie with Rakesh in Residential Café]

Rakesh : Nice pics. When did we took this?

Angelina : Did you really forgot?

Rakesh : Yes! of course!

Angelina : Oooooh, gosh , we took this pics today.

Rakesh : Are you joking?

Angelina : no!, did you really fogot?

Rakesh : Will you evaporate about these pics?

Angelina : Ok.Wc went to dinner tonight at 7 PM and retuned at 10PM.While returning we took selfies.

Rakesh : Where?

Angelina : In the Residential café.

Rakesh : What!, that's impossible!

Rakesh : I am in the office till 10 and just now i retuned home.

Angelina : WHAT?

Rakesh : ok, don't freak out,that's not me and you meet me in the Jeepers Creepers café.

Rakesh : See, i will be wearing black shirt, jeans, and a black hat.

Rakesh : If you see me anywhere, do message me.

Angelina : Ok.

RAKESH IS ON HIS WAY TO JEEPERS CREEPERS CAFE`

Rakesh saw Angelina walking towards the café. He stopped the car and went to meet Angelina.They both met and started talking about what was happened.After few minutes,Angelina goes to washroom. After 5 minutes Rakesh saw her coming from the front door.He immediately asks Angelina why did you come through the front door and she said "I Came just now " .Then they started conversation.......

Rakesh : I saw you going to the washroom

Angelina : No, i came just now

Rakesh : No, i saw you and we discussed about what was happened .

Angelina : No, that's impossible i came just now

Then Rakesh notices that Angelina dress was changed ....

Then he says her to leave now and I'M not in discussion mood

Angelina and Rakesh leaves...

THE NEXT DAY MORNING

Again Rakesh started to chat with Angelina like this..

Rakesh : Where are you now?

Angelina : In home

Rakesh : ok. Meet me at the back woods of my hose at 12 PM

Angelina : Ok

Rakesh : I will wear a blue hat, if not don't talt to me and return to your house

Angelina : Ok

AT 12 PM

Rakesh and Angelina both met at woods and then Rakesh asks her that anyone saw or followed her while coming. She says no. And Rakesh says "Ok, now listen to me carefully , someone is watching us and they are confusing us, so be careful and then.., while Rakesh continuing his words he recieves a message from Angelina stating that she got her tire puncturedand it takes 10 more minutes to come and pls wait.

Rakesh shocks about seeing this message and when he looks up he finds no one ..

And suddenly fog came and someone has it him on his head with a big iron rod. Rakesh was fainted and when he got concious, he finds that he is locked in the a room and tied to a chair.He don't know what is happening around him . He was fully confused .He don't know what to do. He tries to escape but he can't . Then someone with a mask on his face enters to the room and when Rakesh swa him he shouted "WHO ARE YOU?" and "WHY DID YOU KIDNAPPED ME?" but no reply from him and he goes out and locks the door. Then Rakesh finds a small sharp glass piece on the floor and he tries to get it. After so much effort he finally he enties himself and he finds a ventilated door and with a great effort he gets out from there and he rushes to a STD booth and calls Angelina. He tells her to meet him in his office.

 Rakesh goes to his office and freshes up. Suddenly door door bell rings, Rakesh takes his gun and opened the door, He finds Angelina and he points his gun to Angelina and asks her from which number did he call her and she replies "FROM AN UNKNOWN NUMBER" and she asks him where are you till now and he says well, later i will explain. Then he gives her a satellite phone and tells her to contact me with this phone only and don't try to meet me at all.

And he says Angelina to leave fast from here. Angelina left.

From now he decided not to trust anyone. And when he goes out he checks his surroundings whether someone is watching or following him or not.If he gets any doubt he immediately returns to his home.

After somedays he gets some messages from an unknown number

"HELLO RAKESH"

"HOW ARE YOU"

DID YOU GET ANY CLUES ABOUT ME?"

After seing these messages Rakesh tries to finds his location , but he fails to track his location because it is showing different locations every second

Again messages came from that number

"DON'T TRY TO FIND MY LOCATION "

"BECAUSE I AM A GOD"

"O, i am giving you the clue"

"I AM YOUR SCHOOL FRIEND WHO LOVES HACKING AND HOLOGRAM TECHNOLOGIES"

Then, after seeing these messages Rakesh is in confusion, and again a message came

"I AM JOHN CARTER"

After seeing this message Rakesh gets a clarification about what is going around him and now he finds that those people are holograms and he wants to find him.

Then he remembers his intelligent friend Jake. He calls to Jake and explains what was happened and Jake asks two days time to find his location and details.

THE NEXT DAY MORNING

It was around 5:30 in the early morning, Rakesh goes to the park to refresh his mind and suddenly a group of five people were rushing towards Rakesh with knives, Rakesh saw them and runs to save himself but they run faster than Rakesh and they stabs him but Rakesh shocks because he didn't injured and he finds that those people are **holograms.** Then Jake called Rakesh and tells him that **John Carter is dead five years before...........**

After hearing this Rakesh is shocked and confused and thinks in his mind,

"IF JOHN IS DEAD, THEN WHO THE HELL IS DOING ALL THESE"